A Box of Candles

A Box of Candles

by
Laurie A. Jacobs

Illustrated by
Shelly Schonebaum Ephraim

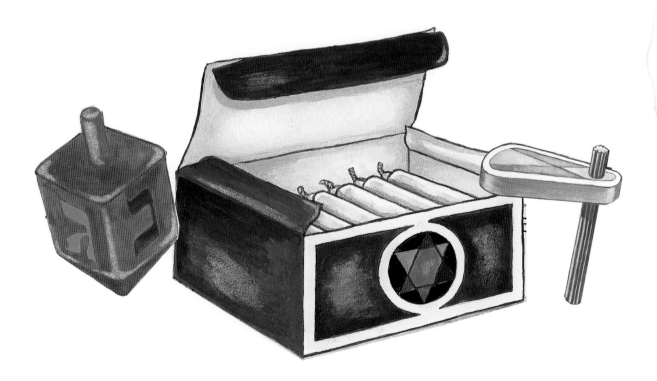

Boyds Mills Press

The author wishes to thank Rabbi Aaron Pels, Temple Hesed,
Scranton, Pennsylvania, for his review of the original manuscript.

Published by Boyds Mills Press, Inc.
A Highlights Company
815 Church Street
Honesdale, Pennsylvania 18431
Printed in China
Visit our Web site at www.boydsmillspress.com

Publisher Cataloging-in-Publication Data (U.S)

Jacobs, Laurie A.
    A box of candles / by Laurie A. Jacobs ; illustrated by Shelly Schonebaum
Ephraim.—1st ed.
[ ] p. : col. ill. ; cm.
Includes a glossary of terms and explanations related to Jewish customs and
traditions.
ISBN 1-59078-169-4
1. Fasts and feasts — Judaism — Fiction.   2. Grandmothers — Fiction.
3. Jews — United States — Fiction.   I. Ephraim, Shelly. II. Title.
[Fic] 22   PZ7.J33637Box 2005

First edition, 2005
The text of this book is set in 15-point Tiepolo Book.
The illustrations are done in watercolor.

10 9 8 7 6 5 4 3 2 1

For Zachary, Hannah, and Sarah
— L. J.

For my family: Lon, Jascha, and Theo.
Your support and love are everything.
— S. S. E.

March/Adar

Oɴ Rᴜᴛʜɪᴇ's sᴇᴠᴇɴᴛʜ ʙɪʀᴛʜᴅᴀʏ, Grandma Gussie gives Ruthie a silver candlestick and a box of candles. In the box there is one candle for each of the Jewish holidays and Shabbats in a year. Shabbat comes every Friday night, so Ruthie's box has many candles.

"When the box is empty," Grandma Gussie says, "you'll be eight years old."

"I hope nothing changes when I'm eight," Ruthie says. "I like everything just the way it is."

On Friday, Ruthie lights the first candle from her box. Ruthie's mother invites their new neighbor, Mr. Adler, for Shabbat dinner.

"You look very familiar," Grandma Gussie says to Mr. Adler.

"I should," Mr. Adler says. "We went to school together. In first grade, you made a mud pie and told me it was chocolate pudding." He wrinkles his nose. "It tasted awful."

"I remember," Grandma Gussie says. She laughs. "Fortunately, my cooking has improved since then."

Every Friday night, Ruthie's family says special blessings to welcome Shabbat. Then Ruthie tells Grandma Gussie about her week in school. But tonight, Mr. Adler changes everything. He tells stories all evening long. No one asks Ruthie about school.

On Saturday afternoon after synagogue, Grandma Gussie goes for a walk with Mr. Adler instead of playing games with Ruthie.

On Saturday night, when Shabbat is over, Grandma Gussie goes to the movie theater with Mr. Adler instead of watching movies with Ruthie.

"I don't like that Mr. Adler," Ruthie says when her mother kisses her goodnight.

"I think he's very nice," Ruthie's mother says. "Grandma Gussie needs a new friend. She's been lonely since she stopped teaching and came to live with us."

"She doesn't need a friend," Ruthie says. "She has me."

One, two, three Shabbat candles burn, and three weeks go by. Ruthie finds lots of reasons not to like Mr. Adler.

He has a mustache.
He wears funny-looking hats.
He whistles.

And he spends too much time with Grandma Gussie.

April/Nisan

The week before Passover, there is a new sound of singing in Ruthie's house. Ruthie is practicing "The Four Questions" in Hebrew. She is going to sing this song at the Passover seder for the first time.

Sometimes when Ruthie is practicing, she hears Mr. Adler whistling the tune next door.

"What a pain that Mr. Adler is," she grumbles. She slams her window shut.

On the night of the seder, Ruthie lights a candle and says the Passover blessings. When it is time for her to sing, she stands up. Everyone at the seder table is looking at Ruthie. She stares at the words in her haggadah. Her hands are trembling. Ruthie has forgotten the tune!

Mr. Adler comes to her rescue. He whistles the song very quietly. Now Ruthie can begin.

"Ma nish tana ha leila ha zeh" . . . she sings. "Why is this night different from all other nights?" She sings the whole song perfectly.

"Excellent job, Ruthie!" Ruthie's father says. "Now we will answer the questions. For many years, we were slaves in Egypt under the pharaoh. Then God led us to freedom. Tonight we celebrate that freedom."

Mr. Adler gives Ruthie a wink and a thumbs-up. Ruthie looks down at her plate.

During the eight days of Passover, Mr. Adler visits Ruthie's house almost every day. He tells jokes. "Waiter," he says, "there's something wrong with my matzah ball soup. The matzah balls won't bounce!"

Even though Ruthie thinks the joke is funny, she doesn't laugh.

One, two, three Shabbat candles burn. Grandma Gussie and Mr. Adler go bowling every Wednesday. When they ask Ruthie to come along, she shakes her head. "I'm teaching myself to ride my bicycle," she says.

One, two, three Shabbat candles burn. Ruthie has been trying to ride her bicycle, but she keeps falling over. Mr. Adler says he can help. He puts a broomstick under Ruthie's seat and holds it as he runs beside her. It is just what Ruthie needs. Now she is riding!

May-June/Iyyar-Sivan

Ruthie rides her bike up and down the street. She waves to the mailman. She waves to the joggers. She does not wave to Mr. Adler.

"Better head home, Ruthie," Mr. Adler says. "It's going to rain."

It is still raining on the first night of Shavuot, when Mr. Adler comes to Ruthie's house for Grandma Gussie's cheese kugel. Ruthie lights a candle and listens to the sound of thunder. One *Boom!* is so loud it makes her jump.

"I wish the thunder would go away!" she cries. She pulls her sweater up over her ears.

"Let me tell you about the terrible thunder at Mount Sinai on the first Shavuot," Mr. Adler says. "It boomed like a thousand cannons. Lightning bolts blazed in the sky. The Jewish people were scared, but they knew something very important was happening. Then God gave them the Ten Commandments — the rules telling them how God wanted them to behave."

The thunder does not seem so loud when Ruthie is listening to Mr. Adler's story.

One, two, three Shabbat candles burn. Mr. Adler is busy working in his garden. Ruthie watches him over the fence. She has always wanted a garden.

"I could use an extra pair of hands," Mr. Adler calls. "Want to help?"

"Maybe for a little while," Ruthie says.

Mr. Adler shows Ruthie how to pick tender new lettuce leaves and pull weeds.

Ruthie holds the hose and splashes water on the green plants. She wriggles her toes in the soft, wet dirt.

When Mr. Adler whistles, Ruthie whistles, too.

"School ends in a few days," Mr. Adler says to Ruthie. "If you like, you could help me in the garden this summer."

"Okay," Ruthie says. "I think I will."

July-August/Tammuz-Av-Elul

The summer days are long and hot. In the mornings, Ruthie waters Mr. Adler's garden. In the afternoons, she sits in the shade on Mr. Adler's porch. Grandma Gussie brings ice-cold lemonade, poppy-seed cookies, and a deck of cards.

While they play, Mr. Adler tells stories about his travels. "Once I was camping in Alaska and got caught in a blizzard," Mr. Adler says. "It was so cold that when I tried to whistle, my lips stuck together!"

Ruthie laughs. "I wish it was cold like that right now," she says. She fans her face with her cards.

Mr. Adler smiles. "A wise man wrote that to everything there is a season, and a time for every purpose under heaven."

He tilts back his hat and wipes his forehead. "This may be the hot-enough-to-fry-an-egg-on-the-sidewalk season, but it brings us the basketful-of-red-tomatoes season in the fall. I kind of like things this way."

Ruthie takes a sip of lemonade. "I kind of like things this way, too," she says.

One, two, three Shabbat candles burn. Mr. Adler takes Ruthie and Grandma Gussie fishing. Ruthie catches a fish with Mr. Adler's rod. Mr. Adler gently takes the fish off the hook and puts it in a bucket of water.

"It's beautiful!" Ruthie says.

"It's a trout," Mr. Adler says. "It would make a delicious dinner."

"Oh, no!" Ruthie cries.

Ruthie and Mr. Adler set the trout free.

One, two, three Shabbat candles burn. Ruthie and her family go to the ocean on vacation. Mr. Adler comes to visit. He and Grandma Gussie show Ruthie how to find hermit crabs and sea urchins in the tide pools.

One, two, three Shabbat candles burn. Summer is almost over. Ruthie plucks ripe tomatoes off the vines in Mr. Adler's garden. She laughs when Mr. Adler bites into one and juice squirts onto his cheeks.

September/Tishrei

Tonight is the first night of Rosh Hashanah, the Jewish New Year. Ruthie helps Grandma Gussie make honey cake for dessert. She puts apples and honey on the dining room table, too.

"Sweet things for a sweet new year," Grandma Gussie says. "What will you do to make your new year a sweet one, Ruthie?"

"I don't know," Ruthie says. "I'll have to think about it."

She thinks about Grandma Gussie's question when she lights a candle and says the blessings for Rosh Hashanah.

Ruthie is still thinking about it the next afternoon, when she walks with Grandma Gussie and Mr. Adler to the pond for Tashlich. Everyone brings pieces of bread to throw in the pond. Throwing bread in the water reminds them to throw away all the bad things they have thought or done in the past year.

Ruthie sees her friend Karen and skips over to join her. "Is that your grandpa?" Karen asks when Mr. Adler waves to Ruthie. "He seems nice."

"No," Ruthie says. "He's Mr. Adler, our neighbor. But he is nice." Then Ruthie smiles. She knows the answer to Grandma Gussie's question.

Ruthie throws bread crumbs in the pond. "These crumbs are all the bad things I said and thought about Mr. Adler last year," she whispers. "From now on, Mr. Adler and I are friends."

Ruthie runs to Mr. Adler and gives him a big hug. "L'shana tova, Mr. Adler," she says. "I hope you have a sweet new year."

Mr. Adler smiles. "L'shana tova, Ruthie. Thank you very, very much."

One Shabbat candle burns, and another week goes by. Ruthie lights a candle for Yom Kippur, the holiest day in the Jewish year. The grown-ups and teenagers do not eat or drink from that night to the next. When Yom Kippur ends, Mr. Adler comes over to Ruthie's house. Ruthie brings him glasses of juice and piles of kugel. Mr. Adler laughs and says, "Please stop, Ruthie. If I eat any more, I'll burst!"

Ruthie and her family build a sukkah in their backyard for the holiday of Sukkot. For the seven days of Sukkot, they eat all their meals in the sukkah. Ruthie even lights her candles for Sukkot in the sukkah.

One night, Ruthie is allowed to stay out late in the sukkah to play cards and eat popcorn with Grandma Gussie and Mr. Adler.

"I like the sukkah season," Mr. Adler says. "The stars shine through the roof. The wind rustles the cornstalks. The air smells of leaves and fruit and flowers."

Ruthie grins. "You know what I like best about the sukkah season?"

"What?" asks Grandma Gussie.

"When my popcorn spills, I don't have to sweep it up!"

Sukkot ends and it is Shemini Atzeret and then it is time to dance with the Torah on Simchat Torah.

That night, as Ruthie and her family and Mr. Adler walk home, leaves crunch beneath their feet.

"Fall is here and winter is not far off," Mr. Adler says. "It's the stay-home-and-light-a-fire season. I'd like someone to live with me and keep my feet warm."

Ruthie stops walking. She frowns at Mr. Adler. "Not Grandma Gussie!"

Grandma Gussie and Mr. Adler both laugh.

"No," Mr. Adler says. "I was thinking about a puppy."

October-November/Cheshvan-Kislev

One, two, three Shabbat candles burn. Mr. Adler names his new puppy Brownie. Mr. Adler and Ruthie try to teach Brownie to sit. Brownie would rather jump around and lick Ruthie's ear or Mr. Adler's mustache.

One, two, three Shabbat candles burn. When Ruthie tells Brownie to sit, Brownie sits. But now he likes to chew — especially on Mr. Adler's hats.

One, two, three Shabbat candles burn. Mr. Adler and Ruthie have taught Brownie to hold out his paw, to roll over, and to lie down. Brownie has also discovered that Ruthie's mittens taste delicious.

One Shabbat candle burns, and another week goes by. It is the first night of Hanukah. For eight nights, Ruthie and her family say the special blessings for the Hanukah lights and light their hanukiah. They sing songs and eat latkes. They also give each other presents.

Mr. Adler gives Ruthie a pair of ice skates. Ruthie gives Mr. Adler a new hat that she made herself. She gives Brownie a bone and a mitten that matches Mr. Adler's hat.

One, two, three Shabbat candles burn. Mr. Adler, Grandma Gussie, and Ruthie go skating on the pond. Mr. Adler ties two milk crates together so that Ruthie can lean on them while she skates. Soon Ruthie is ready to skate on her own. She skates around the pond and waves to Grandma Gussie and Mr. Adler.

December-January-February/Tevet-Shevat

When Ruthie comes home from school, she hears Brownie barking in their kitchen.

"Why is Brownie here?" Ruthie asks. "Where's Mr. Adler?"

"Mr. Adler isn't feeling well," Ruthie's mother says. She looks worried. "He's in the hospital. Grandma Gussie is with him."

That night, Ruthie asks God to take care of Mr. Adler. Her stomach feels twisted up inside.

Five days pass before Mr. Adler comes home from the hospital. But he does not stay home for long. His sister takes him to stay with her in Florida. Brownie stays with Ruthie and Grandma Gussie.

One, two, three Shabbat candles burn. Mr. Adler writes Ruthie a letter. He tells her how warm and green Florida is.

"I hope Mr. Adler does not like Florida too much," Ruthie tells Brownie. "He might not want to come home."

One, two, three Shabbat candles burn. Ruthie misses Mr. Adler very much. Sometimes when Grandma Gussie and Ruthie take Brownie for a walk, they stop at Mr. Adler's empty house. Brownie whimpers.

"I know how you feel, Brownie," Grandma Gussie says. She sighs and pats his head.

One more Shabbat candle burns. Mr. Adler comes home. He has bags of oranges and grapefruits for Ruthie's family and a big new bone for Brownie.

"It's so good to be home," he says. He scratches Brownie's ears. He hugs Grandma Gussie. He hugs Ruthie.

"I'm so glad to see you, Mr. Adler," Ruthie says. "It's been the missing-Mr. Adler-season for much too long."

February-March/Adar

One, two, three Shabbat candles burn. Grandma Gussie helps Ruthie with her costume for Purim.

"This gold dress would be perfect for Queen Esther," Grandma Gussie says. Ruthie tries it on and twirls around the room.

Grandma Gussie smiles. "Ruthie, you look as beautiful as a bride."

Ruthie stops twirling. She has an idea!

"Grandma, I think you would make a beautiful bride. You should marry Mr. Adler. Then he wouldn't have to go to Florida if he got sick again."

Grandma Gussie laughs. Her face turns pink. "Thanks for your advice," she says. "But I thought you didn't like Mr. Adler's mustache or his whistling."

"That was when I was seven," Ruthie says. "Now I'm seven and three-quarters."

One more Shabbat candle burns. A few days later, it is the night of Purim. Ruthie wears her costume to synagogue. Her friend Karen is dressed like a pirate. They listen as the Rabbi reads how Queen Esther saved the Jewish people of Persia. They shout and whirl their noisemakers each time the Rabbi says the name of the wicked Haman.

In the morning, Ruthie's mother fills paper bags with all kinds of Purim treats for their friends and neighbors. Ruthie takes a bag to Mr. Adler.

"Mr. Adler," Ruthie begins. "Don't you think Grandma Gussie bakes the best honey cake and the best cookies and the best kugel?"

"Yes," Mr. Adler says. "She certainly does."

"I think you should marry her," Ruthie says.

Mr. Adler laughs. "When I asked her to marry me in the second grade, she punched me."

"Try again," Ruthie says. "I think she's changed her mind."

It is Ruthie's birthday. She is eight years old. Her box of candles is empty.

"This box looks lonely," she says. "It needs more candles for another year of Shabbats and holidays."

"And simchas and celebrations," Grandma Gussie says. "Like weddings."

"Like our wedding," Mr. Adler says. He grins and takes Grandma Gussie's hand. "Ruthie, you talked us into it."

"Mazel tov!" Ruthie yells. She gives them both a big hug. "What should I give you for a wedding present?"

"I know what I would like," Mr. Adler says. "I would like a granddaughter who calls me Zayde Sam."

"Oh, Zayde Sam," Ruthie says, "I like this getting-a-new-grandfather season best of all!"

Glossary

haggadah — This book is used at the Passover seder to retell the story of the Jewish people's exodus from Egypt.

Hanukah — The winter holiday of Hanukah celebrates the victory of the Maccabees, a group of Jewish fighters, over the forces of Antiochus, a Syrian-Greek tyrant who would not let the Jews live or worship as they wanted. According to Jewish tradition, after the holy temple in Jerusalem was taken back from Antiochus, the Jewish priests could find only enough oil to keep the temple menorah burning for one day. Miraculously, the oil burned for eight days. In honor of the Maccabees' victory and the miracle of the oil, Jews light candles for eight nights in a special menorah called a hanukiah. It is traditional to eat foods cooked in oil on Hanukah, like Grandma Gussie's latkes (fried potato pancakes).

hanukiah — Sometimes called a menorah, this candle holder has space for eight candles — one for each night of Hanukah, plus a ninth space for the candle that is used to light the others. On the first night of Hanukah, one candle is lit; on the second night, two candles are lit; and so forth. On the last night, all eight spaces on the hanukiah are filled with lighted candles.

kugel — A type of pudding. One of the most delicious kugel is made with cheese and noodles.

matzah — This unleavened cracker is made from flour and water quickly mixed together and baked so that no rising takes place. Matzah reminds Jews that in their hurry to leave Egypt and slavery, they could not wait for their bread to rise. Matzah balls are dumplings made with ground-up matzah. They are delicious in a bowl of hot chicken soup.

Mazel Tov — A term that means congratulations (literally "good luck").

Passover — Jewish tradition tells how Jews lived in ancient Egypt for several hundred years until they were forced into slavery by a cruel Pharoah. Passover, or Pesach, is a spring holiday that celebrates the exodus of the Jews from Egypt and their release from slavery.

Purim — The story of Purim is written in the biblical Book of Esther, which is also known as the Megillah of Esther. It tells how the beautiful Esther became the wife of the Persian king. With the help of her cousin Mordechai, Esther used her influence with the king to save the Jews of Persia from the king's advisor Haman, who planned to destroy them. It is traditional to dress in costume during Purim, and to send food and gifts to friends, family members, and people who may be in need.

Rosh Hashanah — This holiday is the Jewish New Year. It is traditional to serve sweet foods on Rosh Hashanah, especially things made with honey.

Seder — The seder is a ritual meal in which the story of the Passover exodus is retold. The idea of the seder is to have the participants feel as though they, too, were slaves so that they can better understand the burdens of slavery and the joy of freedom. To do that, certain foods are eaten at the seder: matzah, a green vegetable like parsley or celery, salt water, a fruit paste called haroset, and a bitter herb like horseradish. The Four Questions ask about these foods and the seder rituals:

Why is it that on all other nights do we eat either bread or matzah, but on this night we eat only matzah?

Why is it that on all other nights we eat all kinds of vegetables, but on this night we eat bitter herbs?

Why is it that on all other nights we do not dip even once, but on this night we dip twice (a green vegetable dipped in salt water and horseradish and then dipped in haroset)?

Why is is that on all other nights we eat either sitting or reclining, but on this night we recline?

Jews eat matzah to remember that they left Egypt in a hurry and did not have time to let their bread dough rise. Jews eat bitter herbs at seder to remember the bitterness of slavery. This is also the reason the green vegetable, which represents spring, is dipped in salt water, which represents the tears of the slaves. The haroset, which represents the mortar the slaves used in building, is dipped in the bitter horseradish. Jews recline at the seder because in ancient days reclining at a table was something only free people were able to do.

Shabbat — Jewish tradition teaches that on the seventh day of creation, God rested. On the seventh day of every week, Jews honor this time with Shabbat, or the Sabbath. Shabbat is a day of rest, prayer, and enjoying the company of family and friends.

Shavuot — A holiday that occurs fifty days after Passover when Jews celebrate receiving God's gift of the Torah. It has become traditional to eat dairy foods on Shavuot — like Grandma Gussie's cheese kugel.

simcha — A happy occasion.

Sukkot — This fall holiday recalls the forty years the Jews spent in the desert after the exodus from Egypt and also celebrates the harvest. During Sukkot, Jews eat in a sukkah, a temporary hut or booth that is a reminder of the huts or booths their ancestors lived in while they were in the desert. Its roof must be made of something that once grew from the ground, like cornstalks or palm fronds.

Shemini Atzeret and *Simchat Torah* — Shemini Atzertet is a one-day holiday that follows Sukkot. Simchat Torah, which means "Rejoicing with the Torah," is the day the last Torah portion of the year is read, followed immediately by the reading of the first Torah portion. It is celebrated with dancing and singing in synagogue.

Taslich — A Hebrew word that means to cast off or throw away. Jews symbolically cast off sins on Rosh Hashanah by throwing bread crumbs into a flowing body of water.

Torah — Also known as the Five Books of Moses, the Torah is Judaism's holiest and most beloved document. According to Jewish tradition, the books were dictated to Moses by God on Mount Sinai.

Yom Kippur — Known as the day of Atonement, it is the holiest day of the Jewish year. During Yom Kippur, teenagers and grown-ups fast and pray and concentrate on apologizing to God for any wrong they may have done, as well as asking foregiveness from each other.

zayde — A Yiddish word for grandfather.

Author's Note

All Jewish holidays and Shabbat begin at sundown. Just before sundown, Jews light candles and say a blessing. For Shabbat they say, "Praised are You, Lord our God. Ruler of the Universe, who has sanctified us by his commandments and commanded us to kindle the Shabbat light."

It is traditional to light two candles for Shabbat and the holidays. Extra candles may be lit for each of the children in the family, or the children may light their own candles. Whatever a family's custom, the candles should be lit in the Shabbat spirit of harmony, reverence, and joy.

There are many beautiful rituals, traditions, and customs associated with the celebration of Shabbat and the holidays. Ruthie and her family are just one example of how to celebrate a Jewish year.